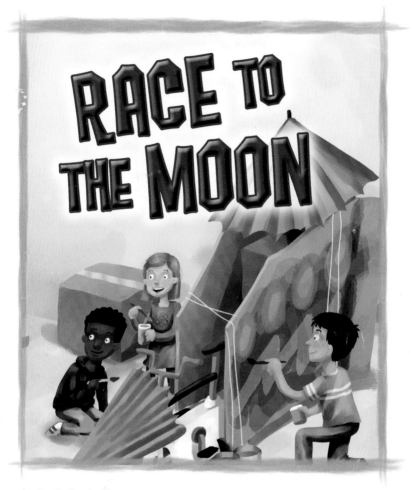

RACE TO THE MOON

Lee Aucoin, *Creative Director*
Jamey Acosta, *Senior Editor*
Heidi Fiedler, *Editor*
Produced and designed by
Denise Ryan & Associates
Illustration © Barry Gott
Rachelle Cracchiolo, *Publisher*

Teacher Created Materials
5301 Oceanus Drive
Huntington Beach, CA 92649-1030
http://www.tcmpub.com
Paperback: ISBN: 978-1-4333-5605-6
Library Binding: ISBN: 978-1-4807-1727-5

Written by
Bill Condon

Illustrated by
Barry Gott

Contents

Chapter One

THE AMAZING IDEA

Rain, rain, rain—it seems like every day of vacation has been wet, and more rain is on the way!

We've played all our video games, watched movies, and surfed online a million times, and now our eyeballs are about to fall out. If we don't find something new and exciting to do soon, we'll be so bored our brains will melt!

Timothy jumps to his feet and says, "I've got an amazing idea. Let's build a rocket ship!"

It's a totally one-hundred-percent awesome idea.

"We can fly to the mall!" Angelina suggests.

"We have to think bigger. Let's fly to an amusement park!" says Madison.

"In a rocket? We've got to think bigger than that!" Timothy grins and continues, "Let's race to the moon!"

I look out the window. I can't see the moon, but I know it's up there somewhere—somewhere really far away from here.

Looking back at my friends, I ask, "It's raining pretty hard. Do you guys think it's too wet to fly a rocket today?"

Timothy shakes his head. "No way! It'll take hours to build a rocket, and by then the rain will be gone."

I can't argue with that, so there is only one thing to say. "Okay, let's do it!"

Chapter Two

ASSEMBLING THE SHIP

Mom pokes her head around the corner. "What are you guys up to?"

"We're going to build a rocket ship," I tell her.

"One that goes to the moon," adds Madison.

"Sounds marvelous," says Mom. "You can work on it in the basement. You'll find a lot of materials for your rocket down there. Come on, I'll show you."

In the basement, Mom leads the way to two cardboard boxes in a corner. Beside them, covered by a sheet of black plastic, are things that are too big to fit in the boxes.

"This is all the stuff that didn't sell when I held a yard sale," Mom explains. "You can use anything you want."

11

"Thank you!" we all cry.

Mom grabs a can of silver paint and some brushes from one of the boxes.

"You can use this, too. I've heard silver rockets are the fastest," she says.

Angelina frowns. "I thought red ones were the fastest."

"Oh, now I'm not sure." Mom digs deeper into the box and finds a small can of red paint. "Here," she hands it to Timothy. "Splash some of this on, too, just in case Angelina's right. Have fun!"

The moment Mom walks out the door, we tip over the rest of the boxes to see what treasures we can find.

13

14

There are a lot of clothes, books, magazines, old CDs and DVDs, some balls of yarn, a broken toaster, a dartboard, and a lot more bits and pieces.

"This is just junk. There's nothing here to help us build a rocket," declares Timothy.

"What about these?" Madison holds up two beach umbrellas.

"They can be the roof of the rocket!" says Angelina.

"They'll keep off the rain, too," I add.

Timothy opens and closes the umbrellas to make sure they're working. "Yeah," he says. "You're right. These will work, and we can use the boxes for the sides of the ship."

Madison lifts up the plastic sheet and turns to us, smiling. "Check this out."

We're looking at an exercise bike. It's old and the seat is cracked, but it still works. I give the wheels a spin.

Timothy congratulates her. "Madison," he says, "you've found our engine!"

Chapter Three

PREPARING FOR LIFTOFF

Mom brings us a plate of her homemade chocolate-chip cookies.

"You can have these now," she says, "or you can take them with you to the moon."

Who cares about food when there's a rocket to build? We decide to take the cookies with us.

Madison and I paint one side of the ship silver, while Timothy and Angelina paint the other side red. We use string to tie the cardboard around the exercise bike, and then we tie the purple umbrella to the bike handles.

Finally, Angelina finds a pack of balloons, and we blow them up and hang them around the ship. Our rocket is looking really cool!

Timothy stands back to look at it. "We're almost ready for liftoff," he says, "but first we need to give our ship a name. Does anyone have any ideas?"

"What about *Starship Madison*?" suggests Madison.

"I like *Starship Angelina*," says Angelina.

"It's got to be *Starship Nicholas*," I say.

"Those are all terrible." Timothy stands up straight and tall. "I think we should name it after our captain... *Timothy's Rocket*!"

"Who made *you* the captain?" we all say at once.

"Obviously, I'm the captain! I'm the one who thought of building the ship, *and* I'm the tallest!" he says.

"But I've got bigger muscles than you," I point out, "so I should be the captain."

"Girls are smarter than boys," says Madison.

"Boys wouldn't even be able to *find* the moon. One of us girls should be captain—probably me, because I'm a month older than Madison." Angelina says.

"That's *so* not fair!" Madison yells.

"Is so!" Angelina yells back.

"Is not!" Madison shrieks.

Just then, Mom walks in.

"The rain has stopped," she says.

"YES! Woohoo!" we cry.

We each grab a handful of chocolate-chip cookies and run outside to play.

The moon can wait. The sun is here.

27

Bill Condon lives in the seaside town of Woonona, Australia. When not writing, Bill plays tennis, snooker, and Scrabble, but hardly ever at the same time. Bill wrote *How to Survive in the Jungle by the Person Who Knows, Pipeline News,* and *The Human Calculator* for Read, Explore, Imagine! Fiction Readers.

Barry Gott lives in Cleveland, Ohio. He has fun illustrating children's books and greeting cards in his art studio. All of Barry's books and cards are guaranteed to make you smile.